Sarah Josepha Hale was a remarkable woman. For forty years, she was one of the most successful magazine editors this country has ever known. She ate grapes every day of her life (for health, she claimed). She nagged Presidents Fillmore, Pierce, and Buchanan and finally convinced Abraham Lincoln to declare Thanksgiving a national holiday. She wrote, in her long, long lifetime, countless articles, books, and poems, including one that began "Mary had a little lamb . . ."

Written in 1830 for a small volume titled *Poems for Our Children,* "Mary's Lamb" quickly became something of a fad. It was set to music, printed on silk handkerchiefs, and produced as a print by Currier and Ives. But, in 1837, when the poem became Lesson XLVII in McGuffey's famous "Reader," its fame was assured. Children in schools all over the country began to recite "Mary had a little lamb . . ."

The poem's exact wording, original spacing, gender, and punctuation from 1830 are used in this edition.

T. deP.

New Hampshire

S.J.H.
DEPAOLA

Mary Had a Little Lamb

Sarah Josepha Hale

illustrations by

Tomie dePaola

Holiday House / New York

For Jean Michie Galloway, Anne Purnell
and all my friends in Newport

The paintings were prepared using transparent colored inks, acrylics, and opaque tempera on 140-lb. Fabriano handmade watercolor paper, which was first coated with gesso. Color separations were made by Capper, Inc. The book was printed by offset on *Moistrite Matte* by Rae Publishing Co., Inc. and bound by Rae Publishing Co., Inc. Designed by David Rogers.

Printed in the United States of America

Library of Congress Cataloging in Publication Data

Hale, Sarah Josepha Buell, 1788-1879.
Mary had a little lamb.

Unacc. melody: p.
SUMMARY: The famous nineteenth-century nursery rhyme about the schoolgoing lamb is accompanied by the music later written for it.
1. Nursery rhymes, American. 2. Children's poetry, American. 3. Lambs—Juvenile poetry. [1. Nursery rhymes. 2. American poetry] I. De Paola, Tomie, ill. II. Title.
PS1774.H2M3 1984 811′.2 83-22369
ISBN 0-8234-0509-5
ISBN 0-8234-0519-2 (pbk.)

He followed her to school one day—
  That was against the rule,
It made the children laugh and play,
  To see a lamb at school.

And so the Teacher turned him out,
  But still he lingered near,
And waited patiently about,
  Till Mary did appear;

And then he ran to her, and laid
  His head upon her arm,
As if he said—'I'm not afraid—
  You'll keep me from all harm.'

'What makes the lamb love Mary so?'
  The eager children cry—
'O, Mary loves the lamb, you know,'
  The Teacher did reply;—

'And you each gentle animal
  In confidence may bind,
And make them follow at your call,
  If you are always *kind*.'

Mary had a little lamb,
Its fleece was white as snow,

And every where that Mary went
The lamb was sure to go;

He followed her to school one day—
That was against the rule,

It made the children laugh and play,
To see a lamb at school.

t Uu Vv Ww Xx Yy Zz

And so the Teacher turned him out,
But still he lingered near,

And waited patiently about,
Till Mary did appear;

And then he ran to her, and laid
His head upon her arm,
As if he said—'I'm not afraid—
You'll keep me from all harm.'

'What makes the lamb love Mary so?'
The eager children cry—
'O, Mary loves the lamb, you know,'
The Teacher did reply;—

'And you each gentle animal
In confidence may bind,

And make them follow at your call,
If you are always *kind*.'

In 1878, nearly fifty years after "Mary's Lamb" was first published, a controversy began. A Mrs. Mary Sawyer Tyler claimed that she was the Mary of the poem and that the real author of the first twelve lines was John Roulstone. Mrs. Tyler said that Roulstone, when a young man in 1817, had presented her with the lines when her pet lamb followed her to school in Sterling, Massachusetts. Roulstone had long since died, and Mrs. Tyler could not produce the original poem, so the controversy soon quieted down—and would have ended, except that in 1925, Henry Ford heard about Mary Sawyer Tyler. He tracked down what he thought was the schoolhouse in Sterling and had it moved to Sudbury, Massachusetts, where it became a tourist attraction. The controversy still continues.

Most of the evidence, however, points to Sarah Josepha Hale as the one and true author. As a matter of fact, in 1878, the year before she died, Mrs. Hale directed her son to write the following: "What can have given rise to the impression that some part of this particular poem was written by another person, she does not know. There is no foundation for it, whatever."

T. deP.
New Hampshire

There are two excellent magazine articles that address the controversy over the poem's authorship: "Mary Had a Little Lamb and Its Author" by Sarah Josepha Hale's great-nephew, Richard Walden Hale, *Century Magazine,* March, 1904, pp. 738–742; and "The Tale Behind Mary's Lamb" by Joseph Kastner, *The New York Times Magazine,* April 13, 1980 (to celebrate the 150th anniversary of the poem), pp. 116–119.